This book belongs to

TORbANDAO

This is the story of a man called Joe,

and what happened in his shoe shop, long ago.

Ready to start? Away we go!

There's something else,

can you guess what?

Throughout this book there's

a slipper to spot.

The Elves
and the
Shoemaker

Nick and Claire Page

Illustrations by Sara Baker

make
believe
ideas

Once upon a shoe shop,
a long time ago,
there lived a poor, old craftsman
called Shoemaker Joe.

Heel and toe,
stitch and sew,
making boots and shoes to go!

Very tired and hungry
was poor, old Joe.
"There is nothing left to eat!"
declared his wife, Flo.

Joe was sad.
Things were bad.
Just some leather was all they had.

Joe cut a piece of leather,
enough for one small pair.
He laid it on his workbench,
and left it there.
He shook his head,
and went to bed.
"I'll start on them tomorrow,"
old Joe said.

Early the next morning,
Flo told Joe the news,
"There's something in the shoe shop:
brand-new shoes!"

Heel and toe,
stitch and sew,
someone's done the work for Joe!

Joe put them in the window,
and can you guess what?
A lady came and bought them.
She paid a lot!
She said, "I'll go and shout
high and low:
buy your shoes from Flo and Joe!"

Joe and Flo had money
and no time to lose.
They bought some more fine leather
to make more shoes.
"Cut it right, leave in sight,
will it happen again tonight?"
thought Joe.

Joe and Flo next morning,
what did they behold?
TWO new pairs of boots there,
waiting to be sold!

14

They were beauties.
They were cuties.
Joe and Flo sold both those booties!

15

Every night, this happened,
just the same.
When Joe left out the leather,
new shoes came.

Sew and stitch,
not a hitch,
Flo and Joe got very rich!

On Christmas Eve, at teatime,
Flo says to Joe,
"Let's wait up and find out
who helps us sew."
So they hide,
eyes open wide.
What surprises there they spied!

18

As the clock chimes midnight,
singing to themselves,
there appear with toolbags,
two small elves.
Tip tap here,
tip tap there,
working in their
underwear!

Two elves with no clothes on
were working in the shop!
When sunrise comes,
they down their tools,
and off they hop.
Heel and toe,
stitch and sew.
"We must make them
clothes!" says Flo.

Joe and Flo made outfits
and left them on the table,
in boxes tied with ribbon
and a label:
"Now we know!
Thank you so.
To our friends,
love Joe and Flo!"

When the clock struck midnight,
Joe and Flo looked on.
The elves unwrapped their outfits,
and put them on.

"What a day!
It's our pay!
Now we can be on our way!"
they said.

And that's where all this ended.
The elves went away.
But Joe and Flo were rich now,
so it was all OK.

Heel and toe,
Flo and Joe,
once upon a shoe shop,
a long time ago.

OUR MOST
POPULAR
STYLE

25

Ready to tell

Oh no! Some of the pictures from this story have been mixed up! Can you retell the story and point to each picture in the correct order?

Picture dictionary

Encourage your child to read these harder words from the story and gradually develop their basic vocabulary.

boot

leather

outfits

ribbon

shoemaker

shoes

teatime

toolbag

wife

Key words

Here are some key words used in context. Help your child to use other words from the border in simple sentences.

Joe **is** a shoemaker.

The elves worked **all** night.

They made new shoes.

Joe **and** Flo were happy.

The elves **went** away.

Make some special shoes

Here's an easy way to make your own pair of very special shoes — just like those from Joe and Flo's shop.

You will need

a pair of canvas shoes (ask Mom or Dad if you can decorate them) • decoration materials: e.g. fabric paint, gold and silver marker pens, glitter paint • masking tape

What to do

1 Wash the shoes well, and leave them to dry completely.
2 While the shoes are drying, think about how you want to decorate them and get together everything you need. Let your imagination go wild! Bright colors work well on white canvas shoes, but black sneakers look great with silver, gold or glitter paint.
3 When the shoes are dry, put them on a table covered with newspaper and get to work. Follow any instructions on the packaging. You may need to be patient and wait for one color to dry before you add another.
4 If you prefer neat patterns, use masking tape to help you make straight lines or neat blocks of color. (Ask a grown-up to help you.)
5 When you have finished, leave the shoes to dry. No one else will have a pair of shoes quite like these!